Everything's Better with a Beard

Si, Willie, Phil, Jase, Jep, and Alan Robertson

Simon & Schuster Books for Young Readers
New York London Toronto Sydney New Delhi

Cowritten by Chrys Howard

SIMON & SCHUSTER BOOKS FOR YOUNG READERS
An imprint of Simon & Schuster Children's Publishing Division
1230 Avenue of the Americas, New York, New York 10020

FIRST EDITION

This book is dedicated to our wives,
who have loved us without beards and
with beards. Hopefully they agree that
everything IS better with a beard!

A boy once asked us,
"It may not be my place,
but why don't you shave those
big beards off your face?

"I don't understand them,"
he went on to say.
"It seems like they would
just get in the way!

"They sop up the soup
and attract lots of dirt
and cover the words
on your favorite T-shirt."

We looked at that kid
and then we calmly said,
"Cut off our beards! Boy,
have you lost your head?

"These beards make us happy!
These beards give us joy!
They're the magic that separates
a man from a boy!

"They're comfy and cozy,
like a winter coat,
or like the hair on Miss Kay's
favorite goat.

"Even the beardless must understand:
growing a beard is God's gift to man!

"Yes, a beard is important,
I hope you will learn.
It keeps lips from chapping
and cheeks from sunburn.

"We show our beards proudly round this old town, and no one can tell when we smile or frown.

"Besides, behind every beard you'll find a great guy:

like Lincoln

and Moses   and Santa   and Si.

"Dogs would look better with beards on their chins.

"They'd look just like us!
We'd almost be twins!

"If the Invisible Man had a beard,
the beard could hang out when
he disappeared.

"Or a truck with a beard!
That sure would be neat.
Any trucker'd be proud to
take that driver's seat.

"And why can't we put
a beard on the Sphinx,

"or that lady who smiles,

"or that feller that thinks?

"This world, well, it would be
a much better place
if we put a beard right on
the Earth's face!

"No, we won't shave our beards.
We'll save them instead,
to make up for men with no hair
on their heads."

That kid was now smiling
from ear to ear.
"You're right!" he exclaimed.
"You *should* keep those beards!"

"Well, boys," Phil said with his
thumb in the air,
"we've made a strong case here
for **more facial hair**."

Miss Kay had been listening;
she'd not said a word,
but she'd thought of something
completely absurd.

She said, "Not *everything's*
better when it has a beard:
a *beard* with a beard—
now, *that* would be weird!"

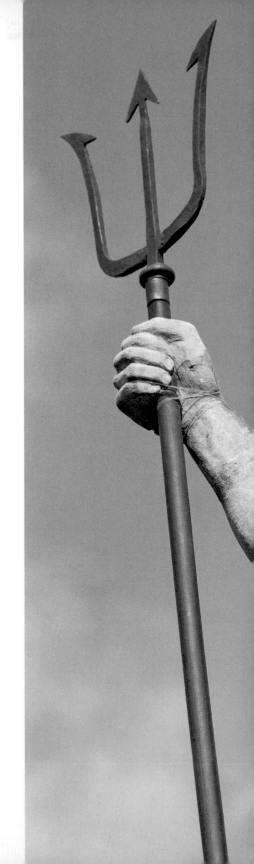

"That's simply not so," we all volunteered.

"Everything's better

when it has a beard!"